Ozlo's Beard

As told by Kingsley Wiggin to Christa Wiggin

Illustrations by Kingsley Wiggin

Chapter 1

Ozlo was happy most days, but not today.
He got out of bed and went to find his mother.

Ozlo's mother was cooking in the kitchen.
"Mother," he said, "why don't I have a beard?"
His mother was busy making a pie.
"I can't talk to you now," she said.
"Go and ask your father."

3

Ozlo's father was working in a noisy mine.

"Father, Father," called Ozlo. "Why don't
I have a beard? You have a beard. Grandfather
has a beard. Why don't I have a beard?"

His father had just found an interesting
green and yellow rock.

"I can't talk to you now," he said.
"Go and ask your grandfather."

Ozlo's grandfather was very deaf.

"Why don't I have a beard?" shouted Ozlo.

"What did you say?" said his grandfather and went to sleep.

No one could tell Ozlo why he didn't have a beard. He went for a walk in the woods to think about it. Along the way he saw a hat on a rock. He went over to investigate.

As Ozlo reached out to touch the hat,
the rock stood up! Ozlo was very frightened.

The creature was very big.

"Who are you?" asked Ozlo.

"I am a rock troll," said the creature, "but you can call me Troll."

Ozlo walked and talked with Troll.

He told Troll that he wanted a beard.

Troll said, "In the high mountain lives
a wise man. We can ask him about your beard."

Troll and Ozlo set off to the high mountain.
Sometimes Ozlo rode on Troll's great shoulders.

Suddenly, Troll and Ozlo found the end
of a very long beard.

"It must be the beard of the Wise Man,"
said Troll.

They followed the beard up and up,
to the very top of the mountain. There they
came upon the
Wise Man.

Chapter 2

"Wise Man," said Ozlo, "why don't I have a beard?"

The Wise Man smiled at Ozlo. "Why do you want a beard?" he asked.

"Well," replied Ozlo, "my father and my grandfather have beards, and I want one too."

"When you grow up, you'll have a beard,"
said the Wise Man.

"But I don't want to wait!" cried Ozlo.

"We thought you could help us," said Troll.
So the Wise Man gave Ozlo a long beard
made of silk. It was magnificent.

They thanked the Wise Man
and started to walk down the mountain.
But every time Ozlo took a step,
he tripped over his beard.

"Drat!" said Ozlo. "This beard is too long."
So Troll put it over Ozlo's shoulder.

As they walked on in the hot sun,
they found a pear tree. The pears were juicy,
and the juice dripped all over Ozlo's beard.
"Yuck!" said Ozlo. "This beard is sticky."

They walked through some woods.
Ozlo bumped into a bush and his beard
caught on some thorns.

"Ouch!" he said.

Ozlo's beard began to hurt more and more.
It became stickier and dirtier. Then it began
to itch.

"I'm very tired. Let's go home," said Ozlo. Ozlo and Troll said goodbye to each other and agreed to meet again soon.

"Thank you for helping me," said Ozlo.

"Thank you for taking me on your adventure," said Troll.

Ozlo's mother and father were waiting
for him and they hugged him tightly.
"You need a bath," they said together.

Ozlo took a hot bath, but he still wished he didn't have a beard. He closed his eyes, and suddenly his beard fell off and floated away in the water.

Ozlo went to bed that night feeling very happy.
"I'm in no hurry for a beard," he thought.
He thought about Troll and the Wise Man
and smiled.